P9-BZG-080

To the
amazing and talented
team at the North Pole!
Thank you for making my
dreams come true.
—CAB

CCA & B, LLC.
3350 Riverwood Parkway SE, Suite 300
Atlanta, GA 30339

https://www.elfontheshelf.com

First Edition
10 9 8 7 6 5 4 3 2 1

Library of Congress Cataloging-in-Publication Data

Bell, Chanda A.
Santa's North Pole: A Christmas Storybook Collection / written by Chanda A. Bell—1st ed. p. cm.

Summary: This enchanting collection features three heartwarming stories shared by Scout Elf™ Joe—Santa's chief storyteller and keeper of the North Pole's legends and lore. In witty, whimsical verse, he also weaves in never-before seen trivia and fun facts about the Scout Elves, Elf Pets and other endearing North Pole characters.
–Provided by Publisher

ISBN 978-0-9600665-4-4

Santa's North Pole

A CHRISTMAS STORYBOOK COLLECTION

by
Chanda A. Bell

Featuring your favorite characters from
The Elf on the Shelf® and Elf Pets®

Contents

My name is Scout Elf Joe;
I work at Santa's North Pole.
I'm his chief Scout Elf,
But I don't do it all by myself.
There are millions of us.
We all make a spirited fuss
Over the world's Christmas Cheer
And other great mysteries here!
We study the myths and the lore
And all the legends galore
That keep the tiny Scout Elves
Perched upon your shelves.

So, come along with me.
Grab cider, hot cocoa or tea.
I have so much to share,
'bout Scout Elves that fly here and there.
They wear their red-and-white suit
With a grin that's clever and cute,
But each has a story to share
That's unique and often rare.

Take Scout Elf Chippey, for one,
His job is not at all done
'Til Taylor chooses to find
Christmas Spirit in his heart and mind.

Then there's Scout Elf Joy
Who helps a young girl and boy
Teach a whole town to be kind
And helps Santa out of a bind.

There's also a boy whose hope
Is lost as he tries to cope
Without his mom for the holidays,
So his elf, and Elf Pets, save the day!

Oops! I almost forgot!
Real cameras cannot be brought
Into the North Pole, so instead,
Santa uses animation to spread
His messages of cheer
At Christmastime every year!
Follow along and let's read
Of elves and kids who succeed!
I'll add a tidbit or two
Of lore and secrets for you.
It will give you a reason
To be a Christmas expert this season!

How is Santa magical at the North Pole?

Christmas Spirit is what he needs
To make all of his missions succeed!

Elf Pets®
Santa's St. Bernards Save Christmas™

Based on the screenplay
by Chanda A. Bell

Christmas is almost here, but something is not quite right in Bellville.

Bob's Helping Hands, a donation center that shares food and clothing with people in need, is in trouble. The shelves are almost empty. Jonah, who runs the center, sighs, "It's been really lean this year."

Still, Jonah doesn't give up! Neither do his kids—Murry, Christa, Kendyl and Brandon. Jonah and Kendyl ask for donations in front of a grocery store. Energetically ringing bells, they call for help, **"We'll take it! Any or all!"** But busy families hurry by or look away.

Only a few coins clink at the bottom of the donation jar. Jonah and Kendyl walk home slowly. Drivers honk and shout. People grumble in line. A hungry man sits alone.

"What happened to Bellville?" Jonah wonders. **"Can anything bring back the spirit of Christmas that used to be?"** Jonah remembers a time when people were more kind and giving.

Did you know that the Christmas Star
Holds the Spirit of Christmas from afar?

Meanwhile, the Christmas Star gleams over the North Pole, and Santa reads the State-of-the-World's-Christmas-Spirit-Update—a moment when the Scout Elves measure the world's Christmas Cheer. Scout Elf Joy Sugar Cookie sings:

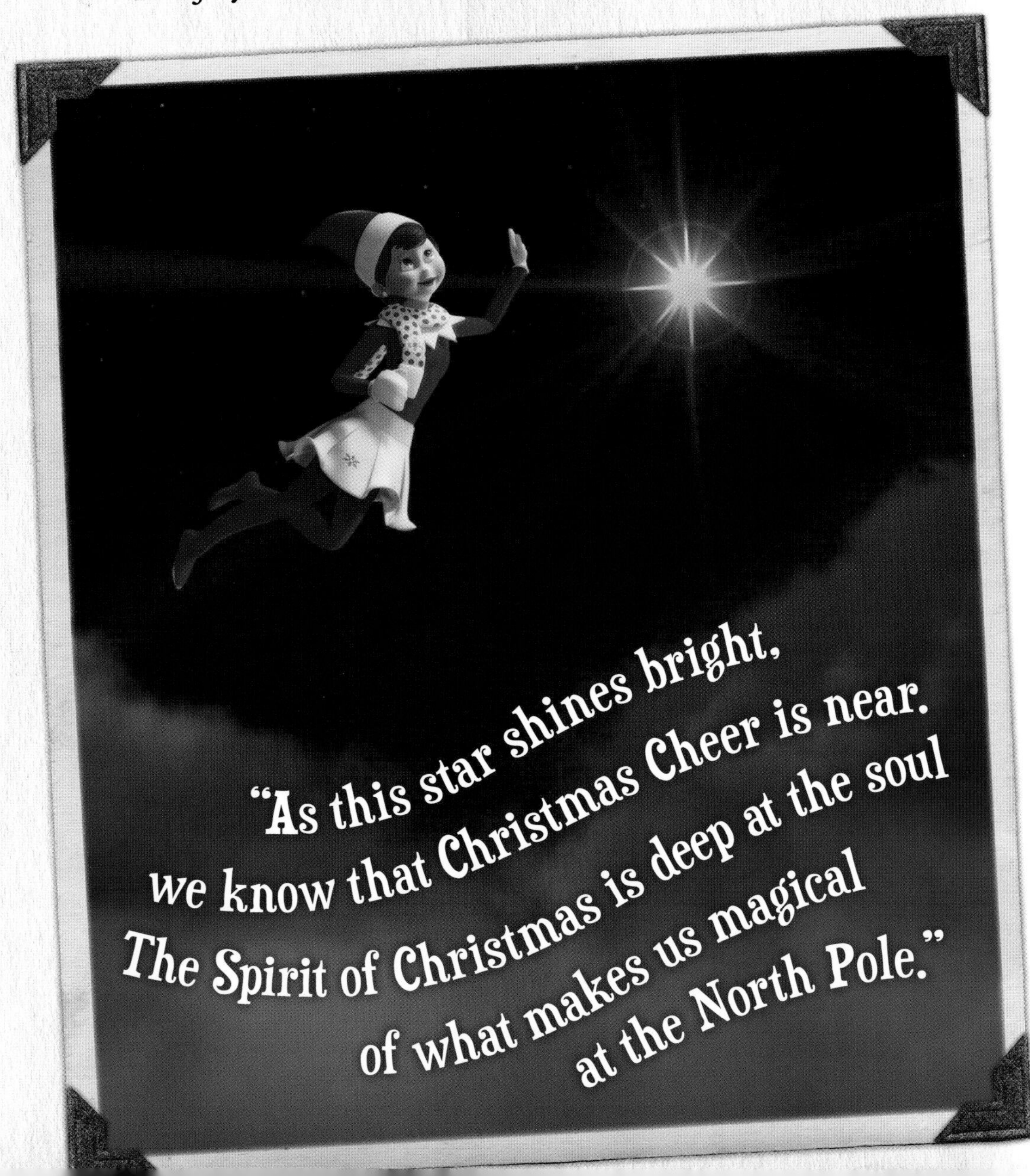

Guess who holds the *Book of Lore*?

Santa reads the update and then gulps. Slowly he says, **"The truth is, my friends, I've seen better years."** The Scout Elves murmur at the bad news, "Without Christmas Spirit, how will toys be made? How will Santa's sleigh have the magic to fly?" Santa opens the *Book of Lore* to find answers.

"When children are kind and choose to do good, their inner light shines," he reads. "And though they won't see it, each time that they try to carry out kindness, their light will supply an invisible trail of holiday cheer."

A deep bark is heard!

Barry the Saint Bernard, the watchdog of Christmas, comes to stand by his old friend, Santa. Then a howling army of Saint Bernard pups rush toward them. Santa knows how the pups can help:

"These pups are here to rescue the soul of the holiday season and save the North Pole!"

Santa's lifelong friend is hairy!
That's right, his name is Barry!
The Alps are where he once helped
Forty people when he loudly yelped—
Bringing aid for those who'd been caught
In a blizzard a snowstorm had brought!

Santa tosses a small, golden charm in the air. It breaks into tiny pieces of light, and each piece floats and bounces until fusing as a golden heart charm onto a barrel around each pup's neck.

It's Christmas Magic!

"Kids will adopt you and give you a name," Santa tells the puppies. "They'll cuddle and snuggle to show they believe, which will give you your magic on each Christmas Eve."

Santa tells the pups to use their brown barrels to gather the light given off by children who show kindness: "Keep it safe and secure. Lock it up tight."

Newly adopted, the pup Sampson snuggles between Kendyl and Murry as they vow to help Santa:

"We promise to do good and carry out kindness to help build Christmas Cheer."

With their older sister Christa, they agree to donate their hard-earned money to help Bob's Helping Hands!

The children shop at the grocery store for Bob's Helping Hands. Their act of kindness changes the grumpy cashier's heart. She donates extra cash, saying, **"Thanks for reminding me what the true Spirit of Christmas is about."**

Lots of invisible Christmas Spirit begins to swirl, thanks to the children and the cashier's thoughtful deed. Kendyl's Saint Bernard pup happily absorbs the Spirit into his barrel to store it, just as he was instructed by Santa Claus.

Their acts of kindness change the hearts of the townspeople in Bellville, too. Soon lots of people arrive at Bob's Helping Hands, bringing bags and boxes filled with food and clothing. Jonah beams, "This makes such a difference. Thank you so much."

The North Pole feels excited, too. Scout Elf Joe shouts the good news from all over the world. **"The puppies' barrels are being filled with Christmas Spirit. Christmas Cheer is on the rise!"**

All the Scout Elves know that Santa needs the special ingredients of Christmas Spirit—faith, hope and love—to make Christmas magic. The Scout Elves and Elf Pets celebrate together. Santa's flight will start on time!

Back in Bellville on Christmas Eve, Sampson and Joy Sugar Cookie gaze at the Christmas Star. Touched by its light, Sampson's barrel opens. The treasure within—**faith, hope and love**—swirls out and is captured by the Christmas Star where it is stored for Santa.

Joy Sugar Cookie, now outside the window, puts her hand against the glass, as if she can touch Sampson's paw on the other side. Christmas Spirit swirls outside, and she flies to join Santa and the other elves on Christmas Eve.

Joy Sugar Cookie bids her family goodbye and is thankful for the people in Bellville and their acts of kindness. It is the key for the extra Christmas Spirit this season. Now, the Spirit will be used to make Christmas magical.

The Scout Elves, Joy Sugar Cookie, Sampson and Santa are full of joy. And as Santa flies into the deep blue night, he chuckles and shouts:

"I offer glad tidings and joy
with a Christmastime blessing
for each *girl* and boy!"

MERRY CHRISTMAS!

How does Santa know who is naughty and who is nice?

The Elf on the Shelf
presents
AN ELF'S STORY®
CHIPPEY'S GREAT ADVENTURE
Based on the screenplay
by Chanda A. Bell

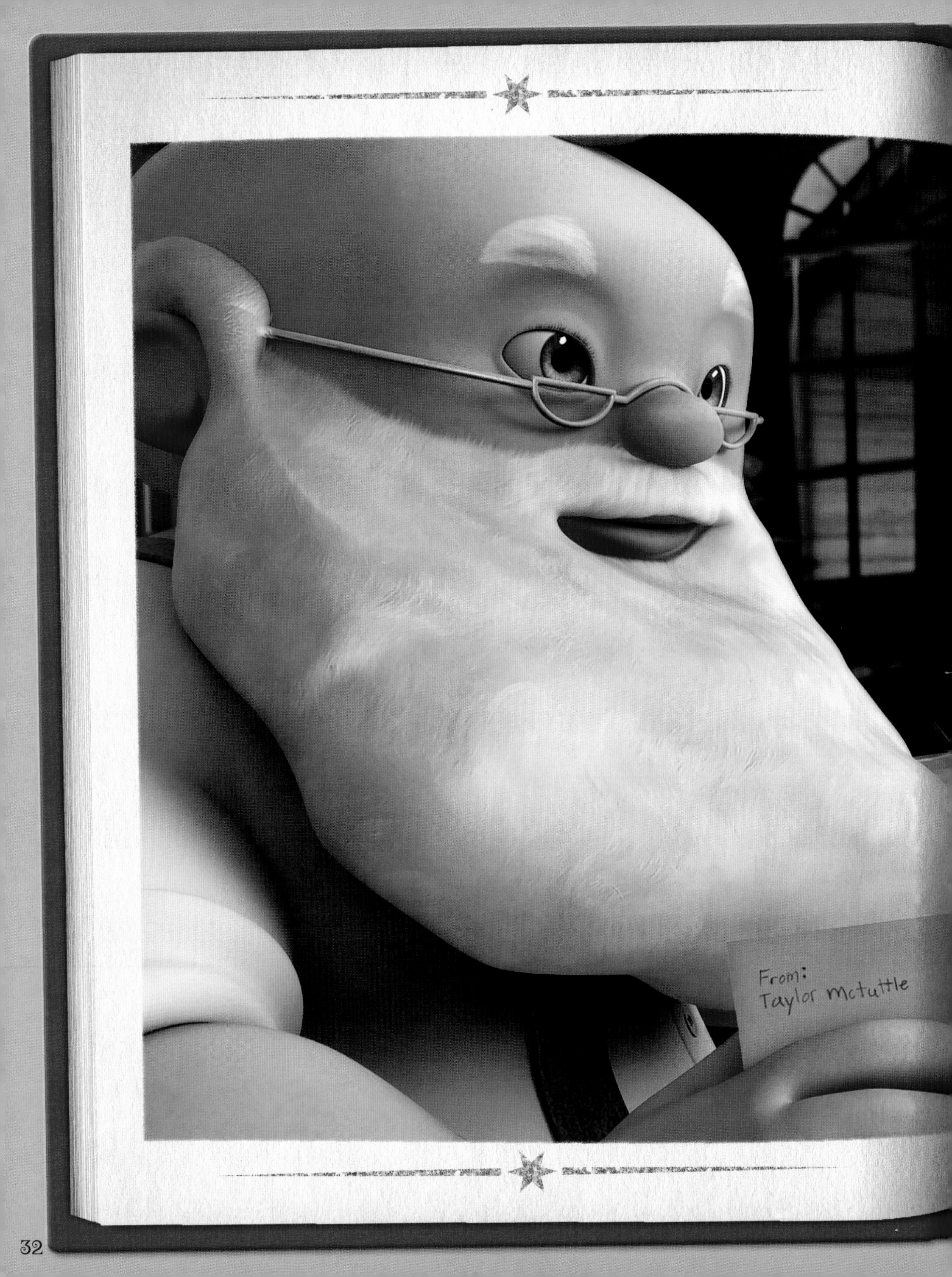
From:
Taylor mctuttle

All of the elves at the North Pole are happy because it is almost Christmastime, and Santa is handing out jobs to all the Scout Elves. One elf is very excited. Santa is sending him on a special mission to visit Taylor McTuttle and his family.

Taylor's twin sisters, Kendyl and Caroline, are overjoyed Santa sent an Elf on the Shelf to them.

"It's our very own elf! Santa sent it to us," they shout happily.

Taylor, though, thinks the elf is just a Christmas decoration and even tries to name him "Stinky Pants." Taylor isn't sure he really believes in the magic of Santa Claus anymore. Finally, the whole family agrees to name the elf Chippey.

The Elf on the Shelf is one kind
Of Scout Elf that Santa assigns
To report back and forth to him
To be certain the star doesn't dim!

How does an elf get its magic?
You give it a name like "Zolo" and "Zajik"!

After getting his name, Chippey realizes he can fly. He flies back to the North Pole to give his first report to Santa. All of the elves are thrilled with their names and their newly found Christmas magic, so they make up a new word to describe how they feel:

EXTRAVAGANZALORIOUS™!

Early the next morning, Chippey flies back to the McTuttle house and hides next to an old picture of Taylor sitting with Santa Claus. Chippey hopes he can remind Taylor of the special visits he used to share with Santa.

Instead, Taylor leans over and asks Chippey to fly around the room to prove Christmas magic is real, but Chippey can't do it because it is against Santa's rules.

When Chippey returns to the North Pole, he is sad. He fears his job to help Taylor fall in love with Christmas again might be harder than he thought. But Chippey's friend, Snowflake, reminds him, **"It's not real belief if they don't feel it in their heart. You can't see Christmas magic. You have to feel it."** So, with more confidence, Chippey returns to the McTuttles.

One day, as Chippey is sitting quietly on a table, Taylor overhears Kendyl talking to the elf.

"Do you really think he is going to fly to the North Pole and take your message to Santa?" Taylor pesters.

"**I believe,**" says Kendyl.

"Me too," chimes in Caroline with a giggle.

Taylor turns and walks towards Chippey, **"I'll believe if I can see your magic."** Slowly, Taylor inches his finger towards Chippey. He is teasing his sisters, but deep down he really hopes Chippey will fly away.

The magic that lives in the heart
Of a Scout Elf can fall apart
And slowly fade away
If handled the wrong way.
You should not touch the elf
That sits upon your shelf.
But never fear, for if you do,
There may be a trick or two,
Grown-ups can use to save
Your elf who is strong and brave.

When Taylor's finger taps Chippey, the small elf falls helplessly to the ground. The twins run out of the room to tell their parents what has happened.

"No—wait!" cries Taylor, running after them.

"I didn't mean to!"

After the children are gone, Chippey lifts himself up off the floor. He tries to fly up the chimney to get back to the North Pole, but he feels so dizzy and weak. He collapses on the ground outside, and his friends have to rescue him.

Taylor feels horrible about what has happened. The entire family misses Chippey, and the twins even worry that Christmas might not come at all! They are terribly upset, but then they remember that Christmas is a time for forgiveness.

Taylor overhears them talking, and he sits down to write the one person he thinks might be able to help, **Santa Claus.**

At the North Pole, Santa is pleased to get a letter from his old friend, Taylor. He knows a certain elf will be glad to hear from Taylor, too. So, Santa goes to visit Chippey in the Elf Emergency Room.

To restore an elf's magic one day
There is no greater way
Than writing a note to say
You're sorry for the way you behaved.

Chippey worries he has failed and let Santa down. "I tried to make Taylor believe," he says, "but I couldn't do it." With a chuckle, Santa explains, **"You can't make someone believe. All you can do is be there. The rest is up to them."** Then, Santa hands Chippey the letter Taylor wrote to say he was sorry.

Fueled by Taylor's belief in him and in Christmas, Chippey finds the extra Christmas magic he needs to get better.

The family is delighted with Chippey's return. Even Taylor welcomes him home.

On Christmas Eve, after helping Santa deliver all the presents, Chippey meets his friends in the sky. As Santa wishes everyone a Merry Christmas, all the elves agree this has been **the best Christmas ever!**

How does Santa travel the whole world in one night?

Based on the screenplay
by Chanda A. Bell

On a cold night at the North Pole, a new Scout Elf journalist, Newsey Noel, thinks about a topic she could investigate as her first assignment. "Children often ask how Santa is able to travel the whole world in one night," she says to herself.

"Santa does have a bit of Christmas magic, but he can't do all of this by himself. "Maybe . . . I could discover the answer myself."

Newsey begins by asking some tough questions of Santa Claus. "Do kids still believe that you're on your way? . . . Can hope still be found? . . . Do you think there could be a problem with 'The Song of Christmas' this year?"

Santa replies, "Why would you think that?"

Newsey knows that faith, hope and love are important ingredients for Christmas Spirit, and without them, Santa can't make Christmas magical. Without Christmas magic, Santa can't travel the whole world in one night.

She wonders if all the sadness and anger in the world will affect Santa's ability to do his job. But Santa encourages her and all her Scout Elf friends:

"There is always so much good; you just have to look for it. No matter how bad things get, hope and faith always win, and never is that belief greater than on Christmas morning once we've made the rounds!"

They all hope for the best and toast the Spirit of Christmas with delicious mugs of hot cocoa!

Meanwhile, Newsey's friend, Captain, arrives. He's there to congratulate her on becoming the North Pole's newest Scout Elf journalist, and he assures her that Christmas Spirit is very high from all he's seen at his family's house. His little boy, Michael, loves Christmas!

Captain is a reporting Scout Elf;
He's actively working as The Elf on the Shelf.

Eventually, Santa reminds Captain, Newsey and all the Scout Elves to do their part and assures them "The Song of Christmas" will live on.

Just then, Scout Elf Joe interrupts, hurrying them along. **"Christmas is almost here, and Santa must be on his way!"** Everyone has a lot to do, and Santa is needed to check on last minute preparations.

In the meantime, Captain returns to Michael's house. Santa, Newsey and the rest of the Scout Elf gang sing and dance their way towards Father Time's Clock at the North Pole. While on their way, they stop to double-check the names on Santa's list, make sure the reindeer have lots of hay and watch as Toy Workshop Elves take the toys from Santa's Workshop to the sleigh. It's a very busy day at the North Pole, and everyone believes it's going to be a great holiday!

Did you know that Father Time's Clock
Needs a password to enter—a secret knock!
It keeps perfect time, never missing a beat;
It's a gift to St. Nick. Isn't that neat?

Back at Captain's house, Michael, an eight-year-old boy who lives with his Grammy while his mom is serving her country in the military, shares some exciting news about Christmas Day.

"My mom is coming home!" Michael cheerfully tells Captain. "I've pretty much waited forever for this! It's going to be the single greatest day of my life!" He also asks for a new snow globe from Santa for Christmas, as he points out his collection. "A new snow globe would be really cool!" he exclaims.

Meanwhile, it's finally Christmas Eve at the North Pole, and all the preparations are complete. Newsey patiently waits on Santa's sleigh in order to investigate firsthand how he travels the world in one night while Santa and his arctic owl friend call out to Noorah.

Noorah is special. You can tell by her tail.
Her name means light, and she never fails
To paint the sky with the mystical lights
Bringing joy to kids on Christmas Eve night!

Noorah hears the call of her owl friend and the voice of Santa on the wind, and she races toward Father Time's Clock. She peers down at Santa when she reaches the edge of the North Pole. Is Santa ready for her to do the job she's done for him for thousands of years?

Santa signals to her, **"It's Christmastime!"**
So, Noorah races across the arctic mountaintops
and uses her magnificent magical tail to spark
the great glow of the Northern Lights.

The lights shield Santa from sight and even pause time, but they can't stay aglow for long by themselves.

When children wake to find gifts left for them by Santa and their laughter fills the air, it forms a sacred song which powers the Northern Lights and keeps them from dying out. As long as children are filled with Christmas Spirit on Christmas morning and carry the hope of Christmas in their hearts year-round, the song will ring out for all the North Pole to hear. Most importantly, it will keep Santa on schedule delivering presents in one magical night.

But for now, the North Pole must wait for this very special song. Instead, they must get Santa up into the air to start his magical journey! Through a beautiful song of their own, the Scout Elves and Mrs. Claus wish Santa, "**Godspeed and a very good night,**" as his sleigh takes flight.

While Santa is delivering presents on one side of the world, it is not quite dark on the other side. So, Michael and his Grammy head out to the store to get a few last-minute baking supplies. To their surprise, they run into their mail carrier, Eleanor. She has a special letter for them, and it looks like it might be from Barb, Michael's mom.

Michael excitedly opens his letter but is quickly dismayed when he finds out that his mom may not be able to make it home for Christmas. Disappointed, Michael runs away in tears. Mail carrier Eleanor picks up the letter Michael left behind and is sad, too, when she learns that his mom won't be coming home for Christmas.

Is there something she can do to help?

Many hours later, on Santa's sleigh and at the North Pole, the Scout Elves begin to hear "The Song of Christmas"! Children's laughter—**the essence of joy**—is beginning to form the magical song that will keep the Northern Lights glowing brightly throughout Santa's trip around the world. Everyone is excited, including Newsey, who continues to learn about selfless generosity and Noorah's magical tail on her journey with Santa Claus.

They are all pleased with Santa's progress and the current Christmas Eve journey when all of a sudden Santa and Newsey reach Michael's house. There, Captain explains that Michael has been so upset about his mom not coming home that he is in despair. He has **lost the ability to believe** that his mom might come home. Newsey and Captain both agree they need Michael to choose hope and find some joy, but it's not looking good.

In fact, Michael's despair is so strong it starts to affect the Northern Lights. They are starting to dim, and "The Song of Christmas" is starting to fail. Santa thinks their best hope might be Noorah, but he wants to use her only as a last resort.

To save Christmas, Santa and Noorah decide she should stay behind and help Michael. Just before Noorah leaps off the sleigh, she grabs a special gift Santa and Mrs. Claus gave her. She has carried it every Christmas, since time began.

When they learn that Noorah has stayed behind with Michael, the Scout Elves wonder, **"What will become of us if 'The Song of Christmas' is not heard?"**

But as Santa and Mrs. Claus introduce Noorah's Elf Pets fox cubs to the Scout Elves, they reveal they've always had a plan: "to team up with children whose hearts are full and grand." Santa sings, **"Anyone can see the truth of Christmas in the lights; it's the kids whose song puts peace on earth each Christmas night!"** He places a special heart charm and snow globe on every little cub.

Newsey and the other Scout Elves feel so silly. They should have known that Santa would have a plan in case "The Song of Christmas" were to ever fail. All kids have to do is shake their fox cubs' snow globes to show they believe; in turn, the fox cubs will remind kids that they are never alone. But what about Michael? How will he get a fox cub?

It turns out that Noorah left him one. So, when Michael woke up early on Christmas morning, he got his own special gift from Noorah and Santa—an Elf Pets fox cub. The book that came with it reminded Michael that "answers don't always come in the way people want them, but they mustn't become fearful or faithless, for that's the great foe of Christmas Spirit. . . ." Michael decides to change his outlook and tells his Grammy they will celebrate Christmas when his mom comes home "even if it's July!" His Grammy hugs him and confirms that **Christmas is a time to be thankful for all that they do have.**

Inside Michael's house, a faint caroling can be heard. Michael and Grammy race to the window. A group of friends and neighbors gather in hopes they can bring a little joy. Little did Grammy and Michael know that Eleanor has gathered everyone together because she was part of a surprise: his mom, Barb, has come home! Michael runs to her and shouts, **"It's a Christmas miracle!"**

But Grammy notices another special gift floating above—**the Northern Lights are dancing in the sky**—something they have never seen before on Christmas morning. Of course, it is a final gift from Noorah as she watches the family celebrate from afar.

Back at the North Pole, Santa and the Scout Elves are grateful that Michael has pulled through and "The Song of Christmas" is restored. Santa finishes his journey and delivers all the presents, but not before they sing and dance in celebration.

Newsey is thrilled because she not only knows how Santa travels the world in one night, but also because she can tell other trainees how the little Elf Pets fox cubs coat the rooftops with snow and spark the glow of the Northern Lights when children fall asleep on Christmas Eve. This will forever keep Santa on schedule, delivering presents in one magical night! **Mystery solved!**

That grandfather clock that hangs on the wall
Just behind Newsey explains it all—
How Santa flies on Christmas Eve
With the help of fox cubs and kids who believe.
It also has a secret door,
A passage to the building of Legend and Lore.

Father Time's Clock Tower

Magical Mail Grotto

Scout Elves' Training Tower

Take a tour of the North Pole!

This is just a tiny glance
Of the North Pole so if by chance,
You'd like to see more just stop by
SantasNorthPole.com. That's it. Bye! Bye!

N
W
E
S
nw
ne
sw
se
Scout Elves in Training Schoolhouse
Santa's Strategy Center and Information Hub
Legends and Lore Laboratory
Elf Pets® Reindeer Stables
North Pole City Center
Santa's Sleigh and Reindeer Stables

My oh my, artists love to tell stories
Of Santa's North Pole and all its glory!
Some use pencils or little line drawings,
Or cute cartoons to get the elves walking.
Some like paint for their trademark look
And bring them to life inside of a book!
How have artists interpreted the characters
of Santa's North Pole over the years?
Chippey the Elf
Character development
Scout Elf Joy
Sugar Cookie
The REAL Elf on the Shelf
reporting Scout Elves!
Santa Claus
NAUGHTY
NICE

Woo-hoo! I'd say, you've learned a lot!
Oodles of smarts is what you've got!
As a helper for Santa, please do your part
To keep Christmas Spirit alive in your heart!
Santa will thank you and so will the pups,
Elves, cubs and reindeer as Santa soars up,
Up, through the sky on his magical sleigh
Filled with gifts that bring joy on Christmas day!